For Mimi, Zen, Stan, and Ember —B. F.

For Helen and the family —B. C.

First published in Great Britain in September 2016 by Bloomsbury Publishing Plc
Published in the United States of America in March 2018
by Bloomsbury Children's Books
www.bloomsbury.com

Bloomsbury is a registered trademark of Bloomsbury Publishing Plc

For information about permission to reproduce selections from this book, write to
Permissions, Bloomsbury Children's Books, 1385 Broadway, New York, New York 10018
Bloomsbury books may be purchased for business or promotional use. For information on bulk purchases
please contact Macmillan Corporate and Premium Sales Department at specialmarkets@macmillan.com

Library of Congress Cataloging-in-Publication Data
Names: Faulks, Ben, author. | Cort, Ben, illustrator.
Title: Watch out for muddy puddles! / by Ben Faulks ; illustrated by Ben Cort.
Description: New York : Bloomsbury, 2018.
Summary: Illustrations and simple, rhyming text warn of the dangers of stepping in puddles, which can be slippery, terribly deep, or
filled with frightening things.
Identifiers: LCCN 2017021021 (print) | LCCN 2017037336 (e-book)
ISBN 978-1-68119-627-5 (hardcover)
ISBN 978-1-68119-842-2 (e-book) • ISBN 978-1-68119-844-6 (e-PDF)
Subjects: | CYAC: Stories in rhyme. | Rain and rainfall—Fiction. | Humorous stories.
Classification: LCC PZ8.3.F2353 Wat 2018 (print) | LCC PZ8.3.F2353 (e-book) | DDC [E]—dc23
LC record available at https://lccn.loc.gov/2017021021

Art created with acrylic paint • Typeset in Bookman Old Style • Book design by Goldy Broad
Printed in China by Leo Paper Products, Heshan, Guangdong
2 4 6 8 10 9 7 5 3 1

All papers used by Bloomsbury Publishing, Inc., are natural, recyclable products made from wood grown in well-managed forests.
The manufacturing processes conform to the environmental regulations of the country of origin.

WATCH OUT FOR Muddy Puddles!

Ben Faulks

illustrated by Ben Cort

BLOOMSBURY
NEW YORK LONDON OXFORD NEW DELHI SYDNEY

Watch out for muddy puddles . . .

because you never really know
what might be lurking
down in the depths below!

You see, puddles can be hiding
so many different things . . .

long-lost soccer balls,
lonely socks,
and underwater kings.

But not **all** muddy puddles
are completely
danger-free . . .

Some are full of crocodiles who'll eat you up quickly!

And tell me, have you ever
been taken puddle fishing?

Look—angry pirates, a giant squid, and—yuck—two frogs a-kissing!

Then this one,
for example,
is the frozen, icy kind.
Tread with care.

Watch out! Don't slip . . .

Too late—
a sore
behind!

Sometimes on the surface
a puddle may look intriguing . . .

Just mind your step,
watch out—
BEWARE!
Looks can be deceiving!

Some puddles will spin you round and round

and make you feel quite dizzy.

Just like a giant whirlpool—
all *twisty*,
whirly,
whizzy.

Others, they are deep.

How deep? You cannot tell.

But one thing is for sure—

if you jump in, it's farewell.

Aaargh!

You'll sink and sink
and go straight down—
straight down through
the planet . . .

tumbling past the
sandstone,
the fossils,
and the
granite.

But the puddle that's by far the worst
(that's if you're very unlucky)
is the one that's home sweet home
to the BIG BAD rubber ducky!

He's fearsome and he's yellow,
so tiptoe, be discreet.
If you disturb the waters,
he'll chase you
down the street.

Though if you're brave, just splash around—
puddles are great fun!

Splishy splashy silliness, enough for . . .

. . . everyone!